Janet Ahlberg

Dedicated to

The Individualist

I am as I am,
And so is a stone;
And them as don't like me
Must leave me alone.

First published 1988 by Walker Books Ltd
87 Vauxhall Walk, London SE11 5HJ

Text ©1988 Iona Opie
Illustrations ©1988 by individual artists

First printed 1988
Printed in Hong Kong by South China Printing Co.

British Library Cataloguing in Publication Data
Tail feathers from Mother Goose.
1. Nursery rhymes in English - Anthologies
I. Opie, Iona   398'.8
ISBN 0-7445-1039-2

Tail Feathers From

MOTHER GOOSE

THE OPIE RHYME BOOK

WALKER BOOKS

LONDON

Foreword

This is a book of cordials and simples. The rhymes and their accompanying illustrations provide comfort for the heart or an antidote to melancholy, fit for adult and child.

Everything under the sun must have its use. The use of a miniature art form like this, small enough to be carried in the head, is that it can cure moments of ennui and black desperation, or grace moments of exuberance or tranquillity. I find myself reciting "Punch, Boys, Punch" in the Underground, while waiting for a train; and I know that a baby in a high chair will swallow food as if mesmerized, under the influence of "Little Popsie-Wopsie". "The Meadow-bout Fields" is especially good for singing, to a home-made tune, in the bath; and "Mrs Burns' Lullaby" will soothe the most intransigent toddler at bedtime. Some of the rhymes can be said ritualistically on special occasions, as when eating Welsh rabbit (see page 42), or, if allowed, jumping on a bed (see page 24). As for rhymes that tell a story, they act as instant spells.

Some families are rich in traditional lore. They enjoy it like aristocrats. They change the jokes and rhymes and songs to suit themselves; their rhymes are sung by particular people ("This is Aunt Susan's knee ride") or to particular people ("We say that to William when he's being stupid"), or at particular times ("We always sing 'Away down East' when we're walking home from the beach – always"). They treasure the family nonsense verses as if they were heirlooms, which of course they are. It is from such families that most of the rhymes in this book have come. The Opie archive has been a repository for rhymes, or versions of rhymes, that have been handed down through several generations, and to which there is at last no heir. The second of the "Two Precepts" was, for instance, sent us by a maiden lady in West Bromwich who had lived by it all her life and did not want it to be lost.

Some of the rhymes were discovered in early English children's books in our collection, or in obscure folkloristic sources. Some have been sent by scholars who found them in early North American children's books. One was overheard in an American bus; another in a Dublin street. Rhymes like these are the common heritage of the British and American people.

They were taken across the Atlantic by British emigrants and acquired an indigenous meaning (see "An Indian Giant's Fishing Tackle"); or, like "The Soldiers' Camp" and "Susanna", they were born in America and have come back to enliven their ancestral stock.

The need to understand the international exchange and flow of children's rhymes, songs and stories (and their illustrations) was one of the principal reasons for our forming what is now The Opie Collection of Children's Literature. This great collection of 20,000 items was built up over forty years by Peter and myself, as a background to our work on childhood. It contains over 800 children's books published before 1800 (a staggering number, considering the odds against their survival), as well as the later story books and picture books, children's magazines and comics. Especially evocative are the books which belonged to famous children: to Queen Victoria when a child, for instance, and the little Darwins, and Emma Hamilton's daughter Horatia, and Alastair Grahame – his copy of THE WIND IN THE WILLOWS was inscribed to him by his father, Kenneth Grahame, who wrote it for him alone.

The Collection represents a unique research tool for anyone studying the history of children's books in any of its aspects, whether literary, social, psychological, educational, or as a hitherto neglected part of the publishing trade. If it goes to the Bodleian Library in Oxford, as I hope it will, it will be kept together as a collection, will be made available to scholars, will have its own separate catalogue, and selections will be exhibited from time to time.

The Collection has been professionally valued at £1 million. I myself am donating £500,000 and "The Friends of the Bodleian Opie Appeal" has been set up, under the patronage of His Royal Highness the Prince of Wales, to raise the other £500,000 by worldwide appeal.

This book is published in aid of the Appeal. The artists who have illustrated it, in styles as various as the rhymes themselves, have given their skills generously and with enthusiasm. The Opie Collection demonstrates, amongst other things, the history of children's book illustration over three hundred years. Now a crown is set on that history by bringing together, in this lovely rhyme book, the foremost children's illustrators of the present day.

Iona Opie

7

PEDLAR'S SONG

Smiling girls, rosy boys,
Here – come buy my little toys.
Mighty men of gingerbread
Crowd my stall, with faces red;
And sugar maidens you behold
Lie about them all in gold.

8

Shirley Hughes

9

A GARDENER

Did you ever see the devil
With his little spade and shovel
Digging taties in the garden
With his tail tucked up?

11

ROISTERING

Whistle or wassail about the town,
  Got any apples? Throw them down!
Cups white, ale brown,
  Barrels made of ivy tree,
Come all you lads and drink with me.
  Up the ladder and down the wall,
Half a peck will serve us all;
  If you'll buy eggs, we'll buy flour,
And we'll have a pudding
  As big as a tower.

12

Anne Dalton

Visiting

Up yonder hill a far way off,

I sammed it up an' donned it on,

Me Uncle John 'e was not in,

So off I went to me Uncle Jim:

So I off wi' me billycock

An' threw it at his head.

The wind did blow my billycock off.

An' off I went to me Uncle John:

Me Uncle Jim 'e wor in bed,

sammed: picked

Helen Craig

15

MRS BURNS' LULLABY

The robin cam' to the wren's door,
And keekit in, and keekit in:
O, blessings on your bonnie pow,
Wad ye be in, wad ye be in?
I wadna let you lie thereout,
And I within, and I within,
As lang's I hae a warm clout,
To row ye in, to row ye in.

keekit: peeped   *pow:* head   *clout:* cloth   *row:* wrap

Robert Burns' wife Jean used
to croon this lullaby to her
children, and the lilt of it gave
the poet a hint for his lyric,
"O wert thou in the cauld blast".

Caroline Anstey.

17

A WASTED JOURNEY

Hie to the market
Jenny came trot,
Spilt her buttermilk
Every drop;
Every drop
And every dram,
Jenny came home
With an empty can.

Jan Ormerod

19

The Eccentric

He kept six butterflies chained in the yard,
    Oh, what an afternoon!

He fed them on beer, tintacks and lard,
    Oh, what an afternoon!

He powdered his hair with pumpkin squash,
And sent his dirty teeth to the wash,

Oh what a, oh what a, oh what a, oh what a,
Oh, what an afternoon!

Richard Warner, a descendant of Oliver Cromwell,
sang – or rather, declaimed – this to us one
afternoon in our house in Alton High Street.
He had learnt it from his nurse, c. 1875.
Each time he came to "Oh!" he thumped the
arm of his armchair with his fist,
and his feet left the ground.

21

HORSES

The huntsman rides a black horse,
The soldier rides a grey;
To plough and sow,
And reap and mow,
To come and go,
And "Whoop!" and "Wo!",
I'll buy a bonny bay.

Chris Riddell

24

MONKEYS ON THE BED

Three little monkeys
Jumping on the bed;
One fell off
And knocked his head.
Momma called the doctor,
The doctor said:
"No more monkeys
Jumping on the bed."

*Overheard on a bus from New York
to Princeton, in 1977. Two boys,
about six and eight, chanted
it repeatedly, serially and
in unison, for the pleasure of
someone aged about two.*

JOHN BOATMAN

Call John the boatman,
  Call, call again,
    For loud flows the river
      And fast falls the rain.

John is a good man, and sleeps very sound;
His oars are at rest, and his boat is aground.
Fast flows the river so rapid and deep;
The louder you call him, the sounder he'll sleep.

26

PUNCH, BOYS, PUNCH

The conductor, when he receives a fare,
Must punch in the presence of the passenjare:
A blue trip slip for an 8-cent fare,
A buff trip slip for a 6-cent fare,
A pink trip slip for a 3-cent fare,
All in the presence of the passenjare.
Punch, boys, punch; punch with care,
Punch in the presence of the passenjare.

A notice in New York street cars, whose potential was realized by Isaac Bromley of the "Tribune". His version was printed in 1875, was set to music, and "ran through the country like pestilence".

A STORY FOR FIVE TOES

This is the man that broke the barn,
This is the man that stole the corn,
This is the man that stood and saw,
This is the man that ran awa',
And this is the man that paid for a'.

NAMES FOR THE FINGERS

Tom Thumper,
Ben Bumper,
Long Larum,
Billy Barum,
And Little Oker Bell.

NAMES FOR THE TOES

Toetipe,
Pennywipe,
Tommy Thistle,
Jimmy Whistle,
And Baby Trippingo.

KNEE RIDE

Father and Mother and Uncle Jan
All rode to market upon a white ram.
Off fell Father, and off fell Mother,
And away rode Uncle Jan.

COMBING THE HAIR

"Comb my hair," said Lady Fair,
"And put some grease upon it,
Not too much of the nasty stuff
Or you'll spoil my nice new bonnet."

DRESSING A BABY

Little man in coal pit goes
knock, knock, knock,
Up he comes, up he comes,
out the top!

FACE PLAY

Knock at the door,
Ring the bell,
Lift the latch,
Walk in!
Take a chair,
Sit down there.
Good morning, Sir!

In January 1956 Alison Uttley, author of the "Little Grey Rabbit" books, wrote to us and sent, among other rhymes, this FACE PLAY used by her mother "who was born over 100 years ago".
"Knock at the door" was a forehead tap. "Ring the bell", a little tug at each ear ("We had never seen a door bell"). "Lift up the latch", eyelid raised. "Walk in!", open mouth and pop a finger inside. "Take a chair" ("She touched my right cheek, on my dimple"); "Sit down there", left cheek. "Good morning, Sir!" ("Finger on chin, she bowed to me").

AWKWARD MOMENTS

PICKABACK
UP TO BED

Up the wooden hill to Blanket Fair,
What shall we have when we get there?
A bucket full of water and a pennyworth of hay,
Gee up Dobbin all the way!

Ron Maris.

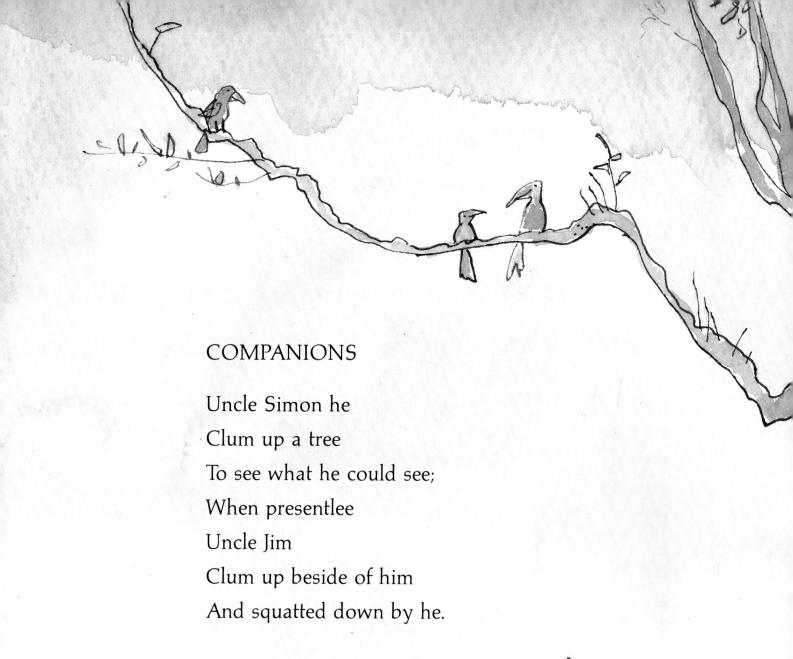

COMPANIONS

Uncle Simon he
Clum up a tree
To see what he could see;
When presentlee
Uncle Jim
Clum up beside of him
And squatted down by he.

33

RIDDLING SONG

Which is the bow that has no arrow?

The rainbow that never killed a sparrow.

Which is the singer that has but one song?

The cuckoo, who singeth it all day long.

Janet Marsh.

Bonny Sailor Boy

I would not have the shoemaker,
For all his work at the shoes,
But I would have the bonny boy
Who wears the tarry clothes.
For he walks upon the plain stones,
He sails upon the sea,
He wears a coat and a hairy cap,
It's a sailor – he loves me!

I would not have the blacksmith,
For all his work in the smiddy,
But I would have the bonny boy
Who has my heart already.
A sailor, he loves me, ma boys,
A sailor he loves me;
And if I live another year
A sailor's wife I'll be!

He
Loves
me

Priscilla Lamont

37

BOOMAN

Ding dong for Booman,
Booman is dead and gone.
Left seven of a family:
Able and Anthony,
Richard and Zachary,
James, Thomas, and John.

Where shall we bury him?
Carry him to London;
By his grandfather's grave
Grows a green onion.

Dig his grave wide and deep,
Strew it with flowers;
Toll the bell, toll the bell,
Twenty-four hours.

LONDON FISHERMAN

There was a jolly fisherman
And he came down from Billingsgate,
To catch a mild bloater,
Or a gay mack-er-el;
When he got to Pimlioco
The wind began to blowco,
The boat went wibbly-wobbly
And overboard he fell.

WELSH RABBIT

The gallant Welsh of all degrees
Have one delightful habit:
They cover toast with melted cheese
And call the thing a rabbit.

And though no hair upon it grows,
And though it has no horny toes,
No twinkling tail behind it,
As reputable rabbits should —
Yet take a piece and very good
I'm bound to say you'll find it.

*The poet Robert Graves knew this in his childhood
and triumphantly recalled it for us, piece by
piece, on a visit to Liss in 1973. BIRD SONG (page 66)
was another he remembered for us on the same occasion.*

Peter Cross

THE GENIUS

When a very little boy
  They sent me first to school,
My master said, though least of all
  I was the biggest fool:
    Such a genius I did grow.

They tried with cakes and cunning
  To put learning in my head;
  But I ne'er could tell which was great A
And which was crooked Z:
Such a genius I did grow.

Arithmetic it puzzled me;
  But as my knowledge grew,
I soon found out that one and one
  When added up, made two:
  Such a genius I did grow.

44

A great musician I became,
  And, as the people said,
Upon the grinding organ
  Most delightfully I played:
    Such a genius I did grow.

Upon my travels I set out
  The English folks to see,
And I found out that they'd arms and legs,
  And head and all, like me:
    Such a genius I did grow.

The Lord Mayor and the Aldermen
  My absence did require –
    They sent me home, for fear that I
      Should set the Thames on fire:
        Such a genius I did grow.

John Burningham

45

AN INDIAN GIANT'S FISHING TACKLE

His angle-rod made of a sturdy oak,
His line a cable which in storms ne'er broke;
His hook he baited with a dragon's tail,
He sat upon a rock and bobbed for whale.

*This giant was, according to American Indian
tradition, resident on Cape Cod. Nantucket and
Martha's Vineyard are said to be formed from
the ashes emptied from his tobacco pipe.
But the lines were originally English.
They appear in an anonymous "Mock Romance"
published in London in 1653.*

TWO PRECEPTS

A little health, a little wealth,

A little house and freedom;

And at the end a little friend,

And little cause to need him.

48

Eat less; breathe more.

Talk less; think more.

Ride less; walk more.

Clothe less; bathe more.

Worry less; give more.

Preach less; practise more.

Graham Percy

49

FISHERMEN'S SONGS

The herring loves the merry moonlight,

The mackerel loves the wind,

Never a fisherman need there be,

Scrub weel yer fresh fish,

Skim weel yer bree,

But the oyster loves the dredging song   For she comes of a gentler kind.

If fishes could hear as well as see.

For there's mony a foul-footed beast   Sooms i' th' sea.

bree: broth   *sooms:* swims

MARCIA WILLIAMS.

51

A Rash Stipulation

The daughter of the farrier
Could find no one to marry her,
Because she said
She would not wed
A man who could not carry her.

The foolish girl was wrong enough,
And had to wait quite long enough;
For as she sat
She grew so fat
That nobody was strong enough.

Babette Cole

53

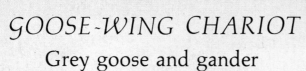

GOOSE-WING CHARIOT

Grey goose and gander
Waft your wings together
And carry the good King's daughter
Over the one-strand river.

one-strand river: the sea

54

"DEFIANCE"

Arise, arise, arumble,

The rats are at the pies!

It doesn't MATTER,

They'll get all the FATTER,

And I will NOT arise.

Louise Voce

THE SOLDIERS' CAMP

Father and I went down to camp
Along with Captain Gooden,
And there we saw the men and boys
As thick as hasty pudden';
With fire ribbons in their hats,
They looked tarnation fine O,
I wish I had just such a one
To give to my Jemimo.

hasty pudden': pudding made in a hurry
fire ribbons: army badges

Louise Brierley.

The Hirdy Dirdy

The Hirdy Dirdy cam' hame frae the hill, hungry, hungry.

"Faar's my gruel?" said the Hirdy Dirdy.
"It's sittin' there i' the bowl;

The black chicken and the grey
Hae been peckin' at it a' the day."

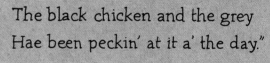

60

He up wi' his club an' gied 'em it o' the lug.

"Peak, peak," cried the chicken. "Will-a-wins!" cried the hen.

"Little matter," said the cock, "Ye should hae gaen to yer bed fan I bade you."

This sinister-sounding story was told in Maryculter, Aberdeenshire, c. 1805. It is less creepy (but also less fascinating) when it is translated into farmyard terms. The shepherd comes back from work and learns that the chickens have been eating his gruel. He hits them over the head. "Chirp, chirp," says the chicken. "Will-a-wins!" ("Lack-a-day!") exclaims the hen. "Little matter," says the cock. "You should have gone to bed when I told you."

Juan Wijngaard

ARISE, ARISE, DOMINO DECREE

Arise, arise, Domino Decree,
Put on thine upsliders and thy downtreaders,
and come and see,
For I have wakened thy Filioc and Filiae;
The white-faced Jenkin has fallen into
the hot popolorum,
And if you don't apply the cold absolution
We shall soon all be undone.

Cold absolution.

Filioc.

Filiae.

Although usually handed down in families as mysterious nonsense, this verse is in fact the culmination of a folk-tale about a young servant girl, hired by an eccentric master who had his own grandiose names for everything and everybody. She must call him "Domino Decree"; his trousers she must call "upsliders", his slippers "downtreaders", his son "Filioc" and his daughter "Filiae". The "white-faced Jenkin" was the cat, "hot popolorum" was the fire, and "cold absolution" was water.
So when, one night, the house caught fire, the little servant had to rouse her master with this long rigmarole; and by the time she had finished the place was well ablaze and they only just escaped with their lives.

THE MEADOW-BOUT FIELDS

O I have been to the meadow-bout fields,
And I have been to the gorses;
And I have been to the meadow-bout fields,
To seek my master's horses.
  And I got wet, and very very wet,
  And I got wet and weary,
  And I was wet, and very very wet
  When I came home to Mary!

meadow-bout: marsh marigold

Inga Moore 65

BIRD SONG

I had a little cock and the cock pleased me
And I fed my cock down under the tree;
And the cock went cockety crow:
Then joined in every neighbour's cock
And my cock belled unto.

I had a little duck and the duck pleased me
And I fed my duck down under the tree;
The duck went quack quack,
And the cock went cockety crow:
Then joined in every neighbour's cock
And my cock belled unto.

I had a little guinea and the guinea pleased me
And I fed my guinea down under the tree;
And the guinea went cook-back,
The duck went quack quack,
And the cock went cockety crow:
Then joined in every neighbour's cock
And my cock belled unto.

guinea: guinea hen

*Another song from Robert Graves' childhood –
see also WELSH RABBIT (page 42). Maybe he
learned it from his Irish father; maybe he
(or his father) gave the refrain its special
magic – one never knows, with poets.*

Patricia Casey 67

A LEARNED MAN

Oh! he knew all about Etymology,
  Hebrew, She brew, jub-jub-ology;
    Syntax, tintacks,
      Hobnails, bootjacks –
He was full as a Pickfords van;
Those who backed and cracked up Edison,
Swore his jaw was more than medicine,
    Simply because,
    People said he was
    A well-learned scientific man.

Pickfords: the famous furniture-removal firm

68

Monday

Thursday

JOHN WESLEY

There was a man, he had two sons,
  And these two sons were brothers.
John Wesley was the name of one,
  And Charlie was the other's.

Now these two brothers had a coat,
  They bought it on a Monday.
John Wesley wore it all the week,
  And Charlie on a Sunday.

Tuesday

Friday

Wednesday

Saturday

Sunday

Colin West 69

Mrs Sparrow

Bring another straw, Cock-sparrow;
I shall lay three eggs tomorrow.
Build a snug nest in the warm thatch –
Bring another straw Cock-sparrow.

The Messenger

Bless you, bless you, burnie bee,
    Tell me where my true love be;
Be she east, or be she west,
    Seek the path she loveth best;
Go and whisper in her ear
    That I ever think of her;
Tell her all I have to say
    Is about our wedding day.
Burnie bee, no longer stay,
    Take to your wings and fly away.

Curiously enough, a "burnie bee" is a ladybird,
"burnie bee" being a corruption of the unidentifiable
"Bishop Barnaby", one of the ladybird's many names.
Ladybirds have long been credited with the ability
to know where one's true love dwells and are
supposed to take flight in the appropriate direction.

71

GRANNIES AND GRANDPAS

Grandfather, grandfather, show your delight,
In comes Betty all in white;
White shoes and stockings, white curly hair,
Isn't she a pretty girl to take to the fair?

Come up an' see yer grannie,
Come up an' see her noo,
Come up an' see yer grannie,
Cos she's all bran' new.
She's got a broken table,
A chair without a back,
A door without a handle
And a window with a crack.

noo: now

72

Old Uncle Luke, he thinks he's cute,
But Grandpa's even cuter;
He's ninety-eight and stays out late
With Grandma on her scooter.

Popular with schoolchildren in the 1950s.
This version was from a boy of eight,
in Hindhead, Surrey.

Robert Crowther

GYPSY

As I went by a dyer's door
I met a lusty tawnymoor;
Tawny hands, tawny face,
Tawny petticoats, silver lace.

RIDING TO MARKET

Ride a cock-horse to Coventry Cross,
To see what Emma can buy;
A penny white cake I'll buy for her sake,
And a twopenny apple pie.

RIDING IN STYLE

Up at Piccadilly, O!
The coachman takes his stand,
And when he meets a pretty girl
He takes her by the hand;
  Whip away for ever, O!
    Drive away so clever, O!
      All the way to Bristol, O!
He drives her four-in-hand.

emma chichester clark

Snorri Pig

Snorri Pig had a curly tail,
A curly tail, a curly tail,
His head was round as the top of a pail,
Hey up for Snorri Pig!

Snorri Pig had big brown eyes,
Big brown eyes, big brown eyes,
And he was jarl of all the sties,
Hey up for Snorri Pig!

jarl : lord

When Snorri Pig met a lady sow,
A lady sow, a lady sow,
He'd smile and bend his knees full low,
Hey up for Snorri Pig!

But when he met another boar,
Another boar, another boar,
He'd tread him into the farmyard floor,
Hey up for Snorri Pig!

Jonathan Heale

*We learnt this from a girl in a tough area of Glasgow in 1975. We think Snorri Pig
must be Scandinavian, because he has the same first name as the Icelander,
Snorri Sturluson, who wrote the "Prose Edda" (saga) in c. 1220.*

79

THE OWL

Once I was a monarch's daughter,
  And sat on a lady's knee;
But now I am a nightly rover,
  Banished to the ivy tree.

Crying, Hoo, hoo, hoo, hoo, hoo, hoo,
  Hoo, hoo, hoo, my feet are cold!
Pity me, for here you see me
  Persecuted, poor, and old.

LITTLE MOPPET

I had a little moppet,
I kept it in my pocket
And fed it on corn and hay;
There came a proud beggar
And swore he would wed her,
And stole my little moppet away.
And through the wood she ran, she ran,
And through the wood she ran.
All the long winter she followed the hunter,
And never was heard of again.

moppet: pet

Anthony Browne.

LOVE

Rowley Powley, pudding and pie,
Kissed the girls and made them cry;

When the boys came out to play,
Rowley Powley ran away.

As I was going up Pippen Hill,
Pippen Hill was dirty,
There I met a pretty miss
And she dropped me a curtsy.

Little miss, pretty miss,
Blessings light upon you!
If I had half-a-crown a day,
I'd spend it all upon you.

STORIES

Margaret wrote a letter,
Sealed it with her finger,
Threw it in the dam
For the dusty miller.

"Dusty was his coat,
Dusty was his collar,
Dusty was the kiss
I had from the miller.

If I had my pockets
Full of gold and siller,
I would give it all
To my dusty miller."

Colin, Colin, Colin,
One, two, three,
Go and ask the blackbird
What's for tea.

First you ask him inside,
Then you ask him out;
Oh my darling Colin,
Please find out.

Charlotte Voake

DINNER TABLE RHYMES

Please, Lord, send summat good to eat:
Not rusty bacon or fatty meat
Or t'wife's sad buns from floppy barm –
Keep me from all digestive harm.

barm: yeast

Little Popsie-Wopsie
Chickabidee chum,
She shall have a piesie-wysie
And a sugar plum.
She shall ridie pie-die
In a coachie-woachie too,
All round the parkie-warkie
With her cock-a-doodle-doo.

A rhyme said to the latest arrival at meal times

Here's good bread and cheese and porter,
  Here's good bread and cheese and porter;
You all may sing a better song
  But you cannot sing a shorter!

porter: ale

Bob Graham.

The Chatelaine

I had a little castle upon the seaside,
One half was water, the other was land;
I opened my little castle door, and guess what I found:
I found a fair lady with a cup in her hand.
The cup was gold, and filled with wine;
Drink, fair lady, and thou shalt be mine!

89

TWO DANCING SONGS

Oh dear mother,
  what a rose I be!
Two young men
  came a-courting me;
One was blind and
  the other couldn't see –
Oh dear mother,
  what a rose I be!

*This is traditionally sung by
Morris Men before dancing
"Lads a Bunch 'em".*

Leatherty patch,
 and leatherty spoon,
My father he bought me
 a pair of new shoon;
One was a thistle,
 the other a thorn –
I think in my heart they
 will never be worn.

leatherty patch: leather to patch
leatherty spoon: probably just for
 the sake of the rhyme
shoon: shoes
*This rhyme was written
in the margin of a nursery
rhyme book, c. 1835, by the
antiquary John Bell of
Newcastle in County Durham.
"Leather-to-patch" used to be
a country dance, something
like a hornpipe.*

WHEN

Once there was a little boy,
He lived in his skin;
When he pops out,
You may pop in.

This little joke is first found in "The Mother's Gift", 1812.
It depends, like others of the genre, on the word "when". There is, for
instance, the Witch Stone at Lowestoft, which is said to go down to the beach
to bathe "when" it hears the town bell strike midnight.

THE CURE

Cockbendy's lying sick,
Guess ye what'll mend him;
Twenty kisses in a clout –
Lassie will you send them?

clout: cloth

*"Cockbendy" was one of the
"odd old songs" that John Buchan's
father learnt as a child and sang
to his children in the 1880s.*

THE WOMAN AND HER PIG

I went to market and bought me a Pig.
But Pig wouldn't goo.
Pig has four legs,   I had but two:
'Tis almost midnight, what shall I do?

I went a little further, and found me a Dog.
Dog wouldn't bite Pig, Pig wouldn't goo:
'Tis almost midnight, what shall I do?

I went a little further and found me a Stick.
Stick wouldn't beat Dog, Dog wouldn't bite Pig,
Pig wouldn't goo:
'Tis almost midnight, what shall I do?

I went a little further and found me a Fire.
Fire wouldn't burn Stick, Stick wouldn't beat Dog,
Dog wouldn't bite Pig,
Pig wouldn't goo:
'Tis almost midnight, what shall I do?

I went a little further and found me some Water.
Water wouldn't quench Fire, Fire wouldn't burn Stick,
Stick wouldn't beat Dog, Dog wouldn't bite Pig,
Pig wouldn't goo:
'Tis almost midnight, what shall I do?

I went a little further, and found me an Ox.
Ox wouldn't drink Water, Water wouldn't quench Fire,
Fire wouldn't burn Stick, Stick wouldn't beat Dog,
Dog wouldn't bite Pig,
Pig wouldn't goo:
'Tis almost midnight, what shall I do?

I went a little further and found me a Butcher.
Butcher wouldn't kill Ox, Ox wouldn't drink Water,
Water wouldn't quench Fire, Fire wouldn't burn Stick,
Stick wouldn't beat Dog, Dog wouldn't bite Pig,
Pig wouldn't goo:
'Tis almost midnight, what shall I do?

I went a little further and found me a Rope.
Rope wouldn't hang Butcher, Butcher wouldn't kill Ox,
Ox wouldn't drink Water, Water wouldn't quench Fire,
Fire wouldn't burn Stick, Stick wouldn't beat Dog,
Dog wouldn't bite Pig,
Pig wouldn't goo:
'Tis almost midnight, what shall I do?

I went a little further and found me a Rat.
Rat wouldn't gnaw Rope, Rope wouldn't hang Butcher,
Butcher wouldn't kill Ox, Ox wouldn't drink Water,
Water wouldn't quench Fire, Fire wouldn't burn Stick,
Stick wouldn't beat Dog, Dog wouldn't bite Pig,
Pig wouldn't goo:
'Tis almost midnight, what shall I do?

I went a little further and found me a Cat. Cat said "Say **PLEASE!**"

So THEN —

The Cat began	The Rat began	The Rope began	The Butcher began	The Ox began
to kill the Rat,	to gnaw the Rope,	to hang the Butcher,	to kill the Ox,	to drink the Water,

The Water began	The Fire began	The Stick began	The Dog began	The Pig began
to quench the Fire,	to burn the Stick,	to beat the Dog,	to bite the Pig,	to goo:

So it's all over now and I'm happy.

*This is the Opie family version, borrowed and altered to suit ourselves. We liked the pattern of the verses
learned by George Sweetman, of Wincanton in Somerset, in his childhood, c. 1842 (printed in "Word-Lore", 1926). His story was about the
buying of a cat – which did not seem right to us, so we altered it to fit the story we already knew, about a recalcitrant pig;
and we added the part about the cat saying "Say please!" because that gives the story a moral.*

Fritz Wegner 95

CHANTICLEER

Oh, my pretty cock, my handsome cock,
I pray do not crow before day,
And your comb shall be made of the beaten gold,
And your wings of the silver grey!

Jill Murphy

PAINTBOX PEOPLE

Mrs Red she went to bed  with a turban on her head.

Mrs White had a fright in the middle of the night;
Saw a ghost eating toast half-way up a lamp post.

Mrs Brown went to town with  her knickers hanging down;

Mrs Green saw the scene and put it in a magazine.

Nicola Bayley

– GINGER –

Ginger, Ginger, broke the winder,
Hit the winder – Crack!
The baker came out to give 'im a clout
And landed on 'is back.

clout: whack

MR BICKERSTAFF

Have you not seen the famed Mr Bickerstaff,
A man in your walks you may chance for to meet;
Sometimes with a cane and sometimes with a thickerstaff,
Dancing a minuet step in the street?

WOE

Charles the First and Ikey Mo
Side by side a-weeping go.
May the tears that they shed
Cast a blessing on my head:
Yankee Doodle, Queen of Hearts,
Mangel Wurzel, Ice-cream tarts.

mangel wurzel: a kind of turnip

An architect in Surrey sent us this in 1956.
His father used to sing it to him and he did not
want it to die out. It is the sort of rhyme that fathers
delight in and is, of course, just exhilarating nonsense.

Benedict Blathwayt.

THE DISGRUNTLED HUSBAND

Janey Mac, me shirt is black
What'll I do for Sunday?
Go to bed and cover me head
And not get up till Monday.

A rhyme from Dublin.

CLEANLINESS IS CLOSE TO GODLINESS

SOAP

JOHN WATSON   105

SUSIANNA

Away down east, away down west,
Away down Alabama,
The only girl that I love best
Her name is Susianna.
I took her to the ball one night
And sat her down to supper;
The table fell and she fell too
And stuck her nose in the butter –
The butter, the butter,
The holy margarine,
Two black eyes and a jelly nose
And the rest all painted green.

Her father died a month ago
And left her all his riches:
A box of stones, a feather bed,
And a pair of leather breeches –
Breeches, breeches,
The holy margarine,
Two black eyes and a jelly nose
And the rest all painted green.

One might think that this had a particular origin –
that it was a description of one particular event.
But it is simply an amalgamation and regurgitation
of several old songs which must have been sung for
at least the past two hundred years. Probably the
name "Susianna" comes from the American version
of 1846, sung by the "Nightingale Serenaders".
("I been to de east, I been to de west,
I been to Souf Car'lina, and ob all de gals
I lub de bes Is my brack ey'd Susianna.")
Schoolchildren now use it, as they use many other
scraps of secondhand song, for skipping or dancing
in rings, and sing it to a tune rather like
"Polly Wolly Doodle". The lines given here
were popular in Edinburgh in 1961.

Martin Handford

GEORGE BERNARD SHAW'S OPUS 1
Dumpitydoodledum big bow wow
Dumpitydoodledum dandy!

G.B.S. sent this to us in 1950.
"I composed this myself," he said, "to sing
when petting our dog Rover. It was my Opus 1."

Barbara Firth

JACK JINGLE

I am Jack Jingle, the very first one,
And I can play knick-knack upon my own thumb:
With knick-knack and padlock I sing a fine song,
And all the fine ladies go dancing along.

I am Jack Jingle, the eldest but two,
I can play knick-knack upon my own shoe.
With knick-knack and padlock I sing a fine song,
And all the fine ladies go dancing along.

I am Jack Jingle, the eldest but three,
And I can play knick-knack upon my own knee.
With knick-knack and padlock I sing a fine song,
And all the fine ladies go dancing along.

I am Jack Jingle, the eldest but four,
And I can play knick-knack upon my own door.
With knick-knack and padlock I sing a fine song,
And all the fine ladies go dancing along.

I am Jack Jingle, the eldest but five,
I can play knick-knack with any alive.
With knick-knack and padlock I sing a fine song,
And all the fine ladies go dancing along.

R I D D

White bird featherless
Flew from Paradise,
Pitched on the castle wall;
Along came Lord Landless,
Took it up handless,
And rode away horseless
To the King's White Hall.

Snow

Without a bridle or a saddle
Across something I ride a-straddle;
And those I ride, by help of me,
Though almost blind are made to see.

Spectacles

Widdicote, waddicote,
Overcote hang;
Nothing so broad
And nothing so long
As widdicote, waddicote,
Overcote hang.

The sky

L E S

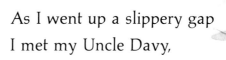

A jumper of ditches,
A leaper of thorns,
A little grey man with
    two leather horns.

A hare

As I went up a slippery gap
I met my Uncle Davy,
With timber toes and an iron nose –
Upon my word he would frighten the crows!

A gun

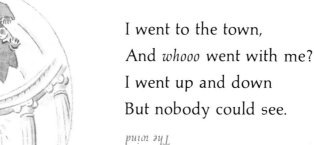

In marble halls
    as white as milk,
Lined with a skin
    as soft as silk,
Within a fountain crystal clear
A golden apple doth appear.
No doors there are to this stronghold,
Yet thieves break in and steal the gold.

An egg

I went to the town,
And *whooo* went with me?
I went up and down
But nobody could see.

The wind

N. JOHNSON.   113

THE GREAT PANJANDRUM

So she went into the garden
to cut a cabbage-leaf
to make an apple-pie;
and at the same time
a great she-bear, coming down the street,
pops its head into the shop.
"What! No soap?"
    So he died,
and she very imprudently married the barber:
and there were present the Chickabiddies,
and the Joblillies,
and the Garyulies,
and the great Panjandrum himself,
with the little round button at top;
and they all fell to playing the game
of catch-as-catch-can
till the gunpowder ran out at the
heels of their boots.

*A nonsense tale (slightly adapted) with which
all families ought to be acquainted. It was
written by the actor Samuel Foote, c. 1760, as
a test for a fellow-actor who boasted he could
remember anything, after hearing it only once.*

JACOB AND JOSEPH

Jacob made for his son Josie
A tartan coat to keep him cosy,
For so 'twas said by holy Mosy –
The very best of men.

Seafarer

I was shipwrecked on a pill-box,
I thought it rather cruel;
After fifteen years of floating,
I landed at Liverpool:

Singing "Radishes a bango,

You-go, I-go,

Chickeracker fango,

Watching the clouds go by."

APPLE HARVEST

Up in the green orchard there is a green tree,
The finest of pippins that ever you see;
The apples are ripe and ready to fall,
And Richard and Robin shall gather 'em all.

Kady MacDonald Denton

MOTION

Fishes swim in water clear,

Birds fly up into the air,

Serpents creep along the ground,

Boys and girls run round and round.

 for Finny

 for Inny

 for Nicklebrandy

 for Isaac Painter's wife

 for Sugar Candy

Index